Angelina Ballerina™

5-Minute Stories

Based on the stories by Katharine Holabird
Illustrations for "Angelina Loves" by Helen Craig
Additional illustrations based on the illustrations by Helen Craig

Simon Spotlight
New York   London   Toronto   Sydney   New Delhi

SIMON SPOTLIGHT

An imprint of Simon & Schuster Children's Publishing Division
1230 Avenue of the Americas, New York, New York 10020
This Simon Spotlight edition August 2022
Angelina Loves illustrated by Helen Craig
Meet Angelina Ballerina, Angelina Ballerina by the Sea, Angelina Ballerina at Ballet School, Step by Step,
Angelina and the Valentine's Day Surprise, Angelina Ballerina Dresses Up, Big Dreams! illustrated by Rob McPhillips
Center Stage illustrated by David Leonard
Family Fun Day, Angelina Ballerina Loves Ice-Skating!, Dancing Day illustrated by Mike Deas

✳ Contents ✳

Meet Angelina Ballerina

Angelina Ballerina lives in the charming Mouseland village of Chipping Cheddar.

Angelina starts each day the same way—dancing!
She practices pliés in her bedroom.

She practices leaps
in the living room.

She practices twirls in
the kitchen.

"Angelina, please be careful!" says her mother. Angelina and her little sister Polly are helping their parents make cheddar pies for a picnic. Today, Angelina and her family are going to the summer festival in Chipping Cheddar!

"Don't forget your dance class," Angelina's father reminds her.

Later, Angelina picks up her bag and twirls out the door.
"We'll meet you at the festival!" her mom says.

Angelina is *very* excited for the festival. The Royal
Ballet is performing. Angelina can't wait to see all the
ballerinas dance onstage!

Angelina dances down the street so fast that she bumps into her neighbor, Mrs. Hodgepodge.

"Watch out, Angelina!" scolds Mrs. Hodgepodge.

"Oops! Sorry, Mrs. Hodgepodge!" says Angelina. Then she leaps and spins all the way to Miss Lilly's Ballet School.

As soon as she arrives, Angelina puts on her pink tutu and ballet slippers. Then she helps Flora tie her bow, and she does warm-up stretches with her best friend, Alice.

Miss Quaver gets ready to play the piano in the studio.

Miss Lilly smiles and says, "Take your places at the barre, little dancers."

Miss Quaver begins to play, and the ballet lesson starts. Angelina loves dancing to the music as she follows Miss Lilly's directions.

"Let's begin in first position," Miss Lilly tells the class.

Angelina and her friends have lots of fun practicing ballet steps together.

Flora leaps in the air and does a grand jeté.

Felicity practices her pliés.

Angelina and Alice do lovely arabesques.

"Splendid!" Miss Lilly cheers.

Angelina's little cousin Henry tries to do an arabesque too, but he falls over and stubs his toe.

"Ouch!" cries Henry.

"Oh no!" says Angelina, and she takes Henry to see kind
Dr. Tuttle.

"Your toe will be fine," says Dr. Tuttle with a smile. "But don't
do any dancing at the summer festival!"

"I know what will make you feel better, Henry," says Angelina. "Let's visit Mrs. Thimble's shop."

Mrs. Thimble's shop is one of Angelina's favorite places in all of Chipping Cheddar!

"Everything looks so delicious!" says Angelina, looking through the shop window.

"I'm hungry!" says Henry.

Angelina and Henry join all their school friends inside the shop. Everyone is buying Mrs. Thimble's tasty cakes.

Angelina chooses a strawberry cupcake, and Henry chooses a chocolate one. They are scrumptious!

"Come on, Henry," says Angelina. "Let's go to the festival!"

Angelina and Henry meet Mr. and Mrs. Mouseling and Polly at the festival. Then they all play games and take a ride on the giant Ferris wheel!

At last it is time for the Royal Ballet performance! Angelina loves watching the ballerinas dance gracefully around the maypole. When the performance is over, Angelina and Henry clap and cheer, "Hooray!"

At the end of the festival, Angelina, Henry, and her family watch dazzling fireworks light up the sky, and then they walk home together.

"What a wonderful day!" says Angelina.

Angelina Loves

Angelina loves . . . dancing with her friends at Miss Lilly's Ballet School. Angelina dances everywhere! She loves spinning, twirling, and leaping.

Dancing makes Angelina
very happy, but dancing isn't
the *only* thing Angelina loves.

Angelina loves . . . her best friend, Alice. Angelina and Alice like to do all the same tricks, like hanging on the trapeze bar and cartwheeling round and round the playground.

Alice knows how to do some things better than Angelina—like really good handstands.

But Angelina never stops trying, even if she takes a tumble on the playground.

Luckily, Alice is a good teacher. She is patient with Angelina and gives her lots of encouragement.

With Alice as her partner, Angelina learns to do really good handstands too.

Angelina loves . . . the fair. But it's hard to do all of her favorite things when little cousin Henry comes along. Angelina loves soaring through the air on the Ferris wheel—but Henry hates the Ferris wheel.

Angelina loves zooming up and down the roller coaster—but Henry hates zooming up and down. Angelina loves the dark and twisty turns in the Haunted House—but Henry hates anything dark and twisty.

Still, when Henry wanders off without her, Angelina gets very worried.

Then when Angelina finds Henry again, she remembers what she loves even more than Ferris wheels and roller coasters. She loves her little cousin Henry.

Angelina loves . . . riding bikes with Alice down bumpy country roads.

When the road gets
a bit *too* bumpy . . .

Angelina is especially glad to have her good
friend by her side.

Angelina loves . . . ice skating.
Before the big ice-skating show,
Henry needs a little extra help.
Angelina and her friends let him
hold their tails so that he won't
fall down on the slippery ice.
But how can they practice
when Spike and Sammy
keep bothering them?

Angelina learns that Sammy loves doing
funny tricks and that Spike
can skate backward . . .

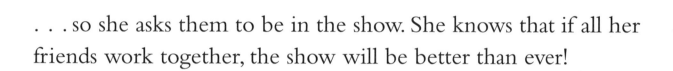

. . . so she asks them to be in the show. She knows that if all her
friends work together, the show will be better than ever!

Angelina loves . . . to work hard and to do her very best. But things don't always go her way. When Angelina gets sick before an important rehearsal, she's much too dizzy to dance. Poor Angelina!

Angelina is very
disappointed, but when she
feels better, she decides to
try again. And this time she
dances beautifully.

Angelina loves . . . her family.
She loves the comfort of her
mother's arms when she's feeling
sick, or sad, or even angry.

She loves the sound of her
father's fiddle. When he plays for
her, she feels like a real ballerina.
And she loves dancing for
Grandma and Grandpa. They are
the very best audience!

Angelina loves . . .
her baby sister, Polly.
Being a big sister isn't
always easy. Polly gets
lots of attention, and
Angelina has to try
very hard not to get
jealous.

Polly tries to do everything
that Angelina and her friends
can do, but she's too little.
So Angelina holds Polly and
promises her that someday,
she'll teach her how to dance
and do tricks, because . . .

that's just what Angelina loves.

Center Stage

The town of Chipping Cheddar was bustling with excitement. The spring festival was just around the corner, and Miss Lilly's Ballet School had been rehearsing for their annual performance of *Mouse Lake* for several weeks.

Angelina Ballerina was the most excited of all. She had been chosen to dance the lead role of Mouse Princess. It was her dream come true!

Every day Angelina skipped and twirled happily all the way to ballet rehearsal.

Then, one day when Angelina arrived, everyone looked upset. "Angelina!" cried her best friend, Alice. "Miss Lilly sprained her ankle! How will the show go on?"

Angelina gasped. What were they going to do?

Miss Lilly arrived, limping into the studio and clutching
Miss Quaver for support.

"I'm afraid I cannot choreograph the rest of the ballet," Miss Lilly
told the class. "Angelina, could you direct the dancers for me this
time?"

"Me?" Angelina asked nervously. "I don't know if I can . . ."

"We believe in you, Angelina!" cheered Alice.

"Please, Angelina?" asked the rest of the dancers.

Angelina didn't like to give up the role of the Mouse Princess, but she knew she couldn't let down Miss Lilly and the dancers.

"Of course I will help," she said.

Just then, Angelina had an idea. She whispered it to Miss Lilly, who smiled and nodded.

"Alice," Angelina called. "Will you dance the role of the Mouse Princess?"

"But you've worked so hard for this role," Alice began, "and I don't think I dance as well as you!"

"I know you can do it!" Angelina said encouragingly.

Alice agreed to dance the lead role, while Angelina would
choreograph the routines. The best friends gave each other a hug.

All of the dancers got into position.

"Plié, then kick!" called Angelina.

The dancers all followed her instructions and worked hard together. Angelina smiled. She was having just as much fun choreographing as she did when she was dancing!

Alice was a little nervous at first, but she kept trying her best. By the end of the day, Alice could do an arabesque just like Angelina!

The rest of the week, everyone pitched in to help prepare for the show. Alice and the other dancers kept practicing their routine.

Henry painted the sets.

Flora and Felicity helped assemble the costumes.

And Angelina kept directing.

Finally, it was the day of the performance!
Angelina and Alice were nervous.
"What if I make a mistake?" Alice asked Angelina.
"What if I let everyone down?" Angelina asked Alice.

Just then, Miss Lilly arrived. "Don't worry, my little mouselings. No matter what happens, remember that working hard and doing your best are the most important things of all," she told them.

The music started. Angelina gave Alice a hug. "You can do it," she whispered.

Alice smiled and leaped out onto the stage. She didn't forget a single step, and she loved dancing as the Mouse Princess.

When the performance was over, Miss Lilly presented Alice and Angelina with two red roses.

"Brava," she cried, "to the cast of *Mouse Lake*; our lead dancer, Alice; and our choreographer, Angelina Ballerina!"

Family Fun Day

It was a beautiful sunny day in Chipping Cheddar. Angelina Ballerina was having breakfast with her family. Mr. Mouseling had made his famous cheddar waffles!

"What a lovely day," said Mr. Mouseling. "Let's go to the park."
"Please, can we have a picnic?" asked Angelina.

"That is a wonderful idea," Mrs. Mouseling agreed. "Would you and your sister like to help pack the picnic basket?"

Angelina's little sister, Polly, jumped up and down with excitement.

"We'd love to!" said Angelina.

"I'll bring our kites," said Mr. Mouseling.

When they got to the park, Angelina and Polly carefully laid out the picnic. There were delicious cheddar muffins, fruit salad, and a cheeseberry pie for dessert.

"Yummy!" said Polly.

After lunch the two sisters snuggled together, and Angelina read a story to Polly.

As soon as Angelina finished reading, she had an idea. "The wind is blowing. Let's fly our kites!" she said.

Oh no! Polly's kite kept getting stuck in the trees!
"Don't worry, I'll help you," said Angelina kindly.

Afterwards, Angelina had another idea. "Let's do ballet outdoors!" she said.

Angelina twirled around the meadow and performed pliés and curtsies.

Polly tried to be graceful like Angelina, but she wiggled and wobbled as she twirled behind her big sister.

"Good practice, Polly!" said Angelina. "Now let's go for a ride on the seesaw!"

The two mouselings raced to the seesaw. It was fun at first, but Polly was always up in the air because she was smaller.

"I know! Let's go to the carousel," Angelina suggested.

They rushed to the carousel, but sadly Polly wasn't tall enough to go on the ride.

Polly walked away and started to cry.

Angelina was
very sorry for her
little sister. Polly
wasn't having
much fun at all!

Then Angelina had another idea. "There are still fun things we can do. Let's play tag! You're it!"

Polly loved to play tag, but she couldn't run as fast as Angelina.

Angelina slowed down and made sure Polly could tag her. That made Polly very happy!

After tag the two sisters got the giggles and fell in a heap on the grass.

Then they heard the ice cream truck, and they both jumped up to get an ice cream. Angelina asked for a cup of chocolate ice cream, and Polly asked for a vanilla cone. As they skipped happily back through the park, Polly dropped her cone. Oh no!

"Here, Polly," said Angelina, offering her ice cream. "You can share mine."

"Oooh, thank you, Angelina!" said Polly.

Angelina put her arm around her sister.

"I will always share my ice cream with you," she promised.

As the sun began to set, Angelina and her family packed up their picnic and walked home. "I had a really nice family fun day!" Angelina said.

Polly giggled. "Me too!" she said.

Angelina Ballerina by the Sea

Angelina Ballerina woke up on a bright, sunny morning with a big smile. Today she was going to the seaside with her family and her best friend, Alice! She could already tell that it was going to be a wonderful day.

Angelina leapt out of bed and changed into her swimsuit. She helped her sister Polly get dressed too. Then they packed their bags with everything they needed for the beach, like hats, towels, and plenty of toys to play in the sand.

"I can't wait to build a beautiful sandcastle with Alice," Angelina said.

In the kitchen, Mr. and Mrs. Mouseling were busy packing a picnic basket full of treats.

"Good morning, girls," their mother said. "There are cheddar scones and milk on the table for breakfast. As soon as Henry and Alice arrive, we'll be ready to leave for the seaside."

A few minutes later, the doorbell rang. "I'll get it!" Angelina cried happily. She ran to the door and opened it. It was her cousin Henry and Alice!

"I can't wait for us to go to the seaside!" Alice exclaimed. "We are going to have the very best time."

A short time later, Angelina, her family, and Alice arrived at the seaside.

Angelina's parents put down the beach blanket, set up the umbrella, and gave Polly and Henry a bag of toys to play with.

"Catch, Polly!" Henry cheered as he tossed a beach ball into the air.

"What should we do first?" Angelina asked Alice.

"Let's make sandcastles!" Alice suggested. "That's my favorite thing to do at the beach!"

Alice fetched seawater with a pail, and Angelina scooped up sand with her shovel. Then they happily worked together, making a beautiful big sandcastle with the wet sand.

Angelina carved a window out of the tallest sand tower. "I would like to live in this room," she said. "Every morning, I could gaze outside at the sea!"

Alice carved a window right next to Angelina's. "This will be my room!" she said.

Angelina and Alice decided to walk along the shore and look for seashells to decorate their sandcastle. They found a perfectly smooth one, a shiny pink one, and even a spiky one!

Alice picked up a conch and held the opening to her ear. "You can hear the ocean waves!" she said, handing it over to Angelina.

Angelina listened closely. Alice was right—it sounded like a whole ocean was inside the shell!

The two friends returned to their sandcastle with their bucket of seashells. Once they finished decorating, everyone came by to admire their work. Henry thought the sandcastle looked just like the Royal Palace!

Angelina and Alice beamed.

After eating sandwiches and resting their tummies, Angelina and Alice decided to play in the water.

"Jump!" Angelina exclaimed, pointing to a wave.

Alice giggled as the waves tickled her toes. "I love splashing in the sea!" she said.

After they jumped in the waves, Angelina suggested they do some ballet routines together.

"Miss Lilly will be so proud that we practiced dancing while we were at the seaside," Angelina told Alice.

Angelina and Alice began twirling across the sand. Then Angelina tried doing a very high leap, and she accidentally landed right on top of the sandcastle!

"Oh no!" Alice cried.

"Oops!" said Angelina. "I'm really sorry."

"We had worked so hard on it," Alice said, sniffling.

"How about we fly our kite?" Angelina suggested. "Or go for a walk along the shore?"

Alice shook her head and buried her face in her hands.

Angelina was worried about Alice being so upset. She remembered that Alice had said building sandcastles was her favorite thing to do at the beach. Even if the ruined sandcastle didn't bother Angelina, it clearly mattered to her friend.

Angelina looked at their seashells, now scattered around in the sand. Then she thought of a surprise to cheer up Alice.

A little while later, Angelina walked over to Alice. "I'm sorry about the sandcastle," Angelina said. "I made something for you, and I hope you like it." She gave Alice a bracelet made out of the seashells they had collected together.

Alice put on the bracelet and smiled at Angelina. "Thank you," she said. "I know it was just an accident. I want to build another sandcastle, but can we have ice cream first?"

"Yes!" Angelina laughed, and the two best friends skipped to the ice cream stand, hand in hand.

Angelina Ballerina at Ballet School

Today was the first day of the school year for Miss Lilly's Ballet School! Angelina had waited all summer for her favorite ballet classes to start again. She wanted to show everyone the new dance move she had created over the summer.

Angelina called her new move the Magical Fairy Twirl. It was the best fun ever. She loved waving her wand in the air and spinning around as fast as she could go. She felt just like a fairy casting a magical spell!

Angelina even had sparkly fairy wings she could wear as a costume. Miss Lilly and the other ballerinas were going to be so impressed.

Angelina packed her ballet bag and rushed out the door. She hopped, skipped, and leapt her way over to Miss Lilly's Ballet School.

Everything was just as Angelina had remembered. She went to her cubby and put on her favorite ballet slippers. Then she pulled out her fairy wand. It was going to be a wonderful dancing day!

Miss Lilly called the class to order. "Welcome back, my little mouselings!" she said. "First, let's start our class with stretches and warm-ups."

After warming up, it was time to dance. "Let's see what everyone practiced this summer," Miss Lilly said.

First she called on Flora, who performed a dainty arabesque. "Bravo!" Miss Lilly said, and everyone clapped.

Angelina raised her hand high in the air, and Miss Lilly called on her to dance.

"I made up a brand-new dance move," Angelina announced. "It's called the Magical Fairy Twirl!"

"A new dance move?" Alice said. "Wow!"

Angelina ran over to her cubby to put on her fairy wings. When she reached into her bag, she was horrified to see that the wings were not inside. In all her excitement, she had forgotten to bring them to class!

Angelina made her way to the front of the class, clutching the wand. Without her wings, she wasn't quite feeling like a fairy anymore.

Angelina took a deep breath and began to twirl, waving her wand in the air. But as she twirled faster and faster, she began to lose her balance!

As Angelina wobbled and stumbled, the wand slipped out of her hands and flew into the air. It soared toward William, who scrambled out of the way just in time.

The next moment, Angelina landed on the floor with a thud.

"Thank you, Angelina," said Miss Lilly. "But I'm afraid I can't allow your new move in ballet school until you've done a lot more practice. I don't want anyone to get hurt."

"That was not magical at all," William muttered, looking annoyed.

Angelina felt very upset as she sat down to watch the rest of the ballerinas. The first day of ballet school was supposed to be the best day ever. Instead, it had turned into an absolute disaster!

After class was over, Angelina walked sadly out the door.

She did not hop, skip, or leap back home.

"How was the first day of ballet school?" Angelina's father asked when she got home.

"It was horrible," Angelina cried. She told him everything that had happened: forgetting the wings, almost hurting William by accident, and having her new dance move banned from class.

"I don't want to go to ballet school tomorrow," she sobbed.

"I understand your hurt feelings, Angelina," her father said kindly. "But tomorrow is a new day. You can apologize to William and Miss Lilly. I'm sure they will understand."

Angelina still didn't want to go to ballet school. The next morning, she walked as slowly as she could.

By the time Angelina arrived at Miss Lilly's Ballet School, everyone was already ready for class. She quietly started unpacking her bag, hoping no one would notice her.

Then Miss Lilly walked over. "Is something the matter, Angelina?" she asked. "It's not like you to be late."

"Oh, Miss Lilly, I'm so sorry!" Angelina burst into tears. "Yesterday was all a terrible mistake. The wand wasn't supposed to slip out of my hand. I wanted to impress everyone with my new move, and instead I made a mess of everything and I disappointed you."

"I was not disappointed in you," Miss Lilly said. "In fact, I was impressed by your creativity."

"Really?" Angelina said.

Miss Lilly smiled. "The Magical Fairy Twirl may not have been the safest idea, but I hope you will keep creating new dances. I know that's what you love to do."

Angelina looked up at Miss Lilly and nodded. Then she hurried over to join her classmates.

"I'm sorry about yesterday," Angelina said to William.

"It's okay," William said. "I think it's fun that you made a new dance move. I made one up too. Want to see?"

William raised one arm and started jumping in the air. "This is the bobbing balloon dance!" he said.

Angelina giggled and joined William. Soon, the whole class was bobbing up and down like balloons.

After class, Angelina walked up to Miss Lilly. "I'm going to keep making new dance moves," Angelina said. "But I'll be more careful from now on. When I'm ready, can I show them to the class again?"

"That sounds like a wonderful idea," Miss Lilly said.

"See you tomorrow, Angelina!" William called.

As Angelina waved back, she was already feeling excited for tomorrow. After all, ballet school was her favorite place to be!

Step by Step

It was a fun dancing day in Chipping Cheddar. Angelina Ballerina was going to teach ballet to her little sister, Polly!

"Before we can dance, we have to warm up," Angelina said to Polly.

"First, sit up tall, and keep your back straight," Angelina said. "Point and flex your toes a few times to stretch your ankles. Reach your hands to the sky, and then try to touch your toes."

Polly tried to copy Angelina, but it was hard to touch her toes!

After a few more stretches, Angelina was ready to teach Polly the five ballet positions.

"In first position you start with your feet flat on the ground. Keep your heels together and turn your feet out so your toes point away from you. Round your arms like this.

"For second position take a small step sideways with your right foot. Hold your arms out to the side, angled slightly down, with your palms facing down.

"Now for third position, slide the heel of your right foot until it's near the middle of your left foot. Then keep your left arm out wide and bring your right arm down so it is in front of your body again and rounded like it was in first position."

Polly smiled. She was having a lot of fun!

"For fourth position step forward with your right foot so that
there's a space between your feet, but they're still turned out.
Keep your right arm where it was last time, but the arm that you
held out wide should now be rounded and raised above your
head," Angelina said.

"Next, let's try fifth position. This time you slide your right forward foot back so that the side of it is touching your left foot, with no space between them. Bring the heel of each foot next to the toes of the other foot. Now bring your right arm above your head so both arms are rounded and held high."

"Yay! I can do it!" Polly cheered.

"Now let's do a plié, which means 'to bend' in French," Angelina instructed.

"We'll start with our feet in first position, with our heels on the ground and our feet turned outward.

"To do a plié, you just bend your knees, keeping them pointed outward. Miss Lilly says to imagine making a diamond shape with your legs!

"Now let's do an arabesque. Stand on one leg and stretch your other leg behind you, keeping it straight. Then lift one arm up high and hold the other arm straight in mid-air. I try to make a straight line from the tip of my raised arm's fingers to the end of my raised leg's toes.

"You're doing great, Polly!" Angelina exclaimed. "I think you're ready to try a grand jeté. It is a big leap in the air. Run and leap forward as high and far as you can with one leg in front of you and the other leg behind you."

Polly tried to leap, but she was a bit wobbly.

"It was hard for me too at first, but now it is easier. Ballet is about practice," Angelina told her. "It will get a little easier each time you try."

Angelina and Polly had so much fun doing ballet together that they decided to invite Angelina's best friend Alice and cousin Henry over to dance too.

Polly grinned as she danced next to Angelina. It had been a great ballet day!

Angelina Ballerina Loves Ice-Skating!

Angelina woke up on a beautiful winter morning. She leapt out of bed and looked out the window. "It's snowing!" she cried happily. "And today is the first day of winter! Isn't that just perfect?"

The first day of winter meant that Miller's Pond was officially open for ice-skating. Angelina loved dancing, so ice-skating was also one of her favorite activities!

Angelina and her sister, Polly, put on sweaters and their warmest coats. Angelina also found her favorite green scarf. "I think we're just about ready!" she said with a smile.

Just then, the doorbell rang. Angelina ran downstairs.
Her friends must have stopped by so they could walk to Miller's
Pond together.

Felicity, Flora, and Alice were standing at the front door. They didn't look very happy.

"Angelina!" Alice cried. "Miller's Pond is closed today. It is snowing too much outside!"

Angelina's face fell. "Oh no! I was looking forward to practicing arabesques on the ice!" she said.

Angelina's mother called all the girls into the kitchen. "There's a blizzard coming," she said. "I'm afraid you'll have to stay inside today. I'll call everyone's parents and let them know you can stay here until it stops snowing."

Angelina was so disappointed. But then she started thinking about how she could have fun with her friends inside. "Let's have an arts-and-crafts day!" she suggested. "We can make decorations for Miller's Pond when it reopens!"

Flora, Felicity, and Alice all thought that was a great idea.

They raced up to Angelina's room.

"We can make garlands of paper snowflakes to hang near the ice rink," Angelina said.

"Oooh!" exclaimed Felicity. "And we can use silver tinsel to make icicles!"

Everyone got to work. Angelina and Alice carefully cut snowflake shapes out of thick white paper.

Felicity wound strands of tinsel together to make icicles.

Flora made fluffy snowmen out of cotton balls.

Angelina's mother made hot cocoa for the mouselings. It was very yummy!

By the time the mouselings had finished everything, the snow had stopped and it was time for everyone to go home. Angelina got into her coziest pajamas and drifted off to sleep.

The next day, Angelina woke up to a beautiful and sunny day. "Good morning," her mother said. "I have wonderful news for you. The ice rink is open today!"

Angelina and her friends gathered at Miller's Pond to decorate the rink. Felicity hung her tinsel icicles from snow-covered branches. Angelina and Alice strung their snowflake garland around the entire rink. Flora decorated the bushes with her cotton-ball snowmen.

Soon many townspeople started to gather at the ice rink.

"Why, Angelina," Mrs. Thimble said. "What lovely decorations!"

"Thank you!" Angelina beamed.

The mouselings all put on their ice skates and twirled gracefully around the rink.

"What a wonderful beginning to the winter!" Angelina cheered.

Angelina and the Valentine's Day Surprise

It was Valentine's Day in Chipping Cheddar! There were pink and red decorations all over the village, and Angelina had baked cookies and made valentine cards for her friends and family. She couldn't wait to celebrate.

To Miss Lilly

"I love Valentine's Day!" Angelina exclaimed as she packed her bag full of goodies and cards.

I love having you as my ballet teacher!
- Angelina xxx

Then Angelina skipped through the village to her grandparents' house. Angelina always had fun visiting her grandparents. She would bake cheesy cheddar scones with Grandma and practice her dance steps and curtsies with Grandpa.

Angelina proudly gave her grandparents her handmade valentine.

"How lovely!" said Grandma.

"Thank you, dear Angelina!" said
Grandpa.

They hugged Angelina, and she
blew them a kiss and skipped away.

Next, Angelina danced over to the village square
to meet her best friend, Alice.

They practiced twirling in heart shapes and
shared some Valentine's Day cookies.

Angelina loved dancing and giggling with Alice.

"Here's an extra sparkly valentine for my extra sparkly friend," Angelina said.

To Alice

Roses are red,
violets are blue.
I'm so lucky to have
a best friend like you!
Love, Angelina

On her way home, Angelina stopped by Mrs. Thimble's shop. Angelina loved browsing in the store and looking at all the pretty ribbons and costumes.

Angelina had wrapped the valentine
and cookie for Mrs. Thimble in a
bright pink bag she had sewed herself.
"Happy Valentine's Day!" Angelina
said as she gave Mrs. Thimble her
valentine.

When she stepped outside Mrs. Thimble's shop,
Angelina saw her cousin Henry. She loved playing
and dancing with her sweet little cousin, so she had
made a valentine for him too.

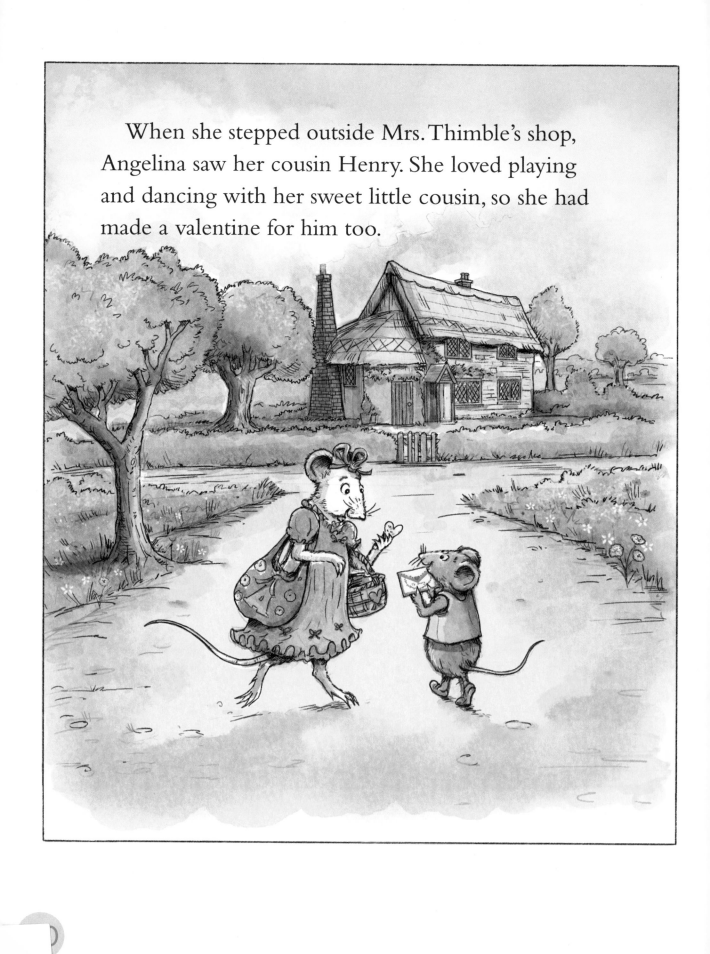

"Henry, wait!" Angelina said. "I have a valentine for you."

"You do?" asked Henry. "Thanks, Angelina!"

To Henry

You may be small... but you have the biggest heart! Love and hugs, Angelina xx

Angelina's bag was empty now. She had delivered all her valentines! She felt happy, but also a little sad, too. She didn't want Valentine's Day to ever end!

When she got home, Angelina saw a bunch of beautiful valentines on the kitchen table. She couldn't believe it: They were all for her!

Violets are red,
roses are blue,
I'm lucky you're my friend
and dance partner too!
Alice

HAPPY VALENTINE'S DAY
2 THE COUSIN I LOOK
UP 2 THE MOST!
HENRY x x x

To our favorite baking partner
and sweetest granddaughter—
we love you!
Grandma and Grandpa
Mouseling xoxo

To our favorite little
dancing mouseling:
Happy Valentine's Day!
Mom and Dad and Polly
xoxo

LOVE YOU

Happy Heart Day
to the ballerina
with the most heart!
Miss Lilly

To Angelina
x

She just had
one more extra-
special valentine
to write. . . .

To you

Will you be my
valentine?
Love,
Angelina X

Angelina did a pirouette in celebration. This really had been the best Valentine's Day ever!

Angelina Ballerina Dresses Up

Angelina Ballerina loves to spend the day with Grandma and Grandpa Mouseling. They have so much fun together!

Whenever Angelina visits, Grandma Mouseling lets Angelina try on her straw hat with flowers on the brim. Then Angelina puts on a special apron that's just her size, and she helps Grandpa and Grandma make cheddar-cheese pies for lunch.

Grandpa and Angelina choose lovely roses to put in the flower vase, and Angelina helps set the table for lunch. While they eat, they talk about plans for the afternoon.

Angelina asks, "Please, can I play dress-up?" and Grandpa and Grandma smile.

Angelina and Grandma open a very special old trunk. Inside, there are dresses and shoes and gloves and hats that Grandma used to wear when she was a little mouseling.

Angelina tries on a beautiful party dress. "My goodness," Grandma says. "You look like a princess!"

"I sometimes play dress-up at Miss Lilly's house, too," Angelina tells Grandma.

Miss Lilly is Angelina's ballet teacher. She is very kind, and she once let Angelina and Alice, who is Angelina's best friend, try on her collection of ballet costumes, tutus, and even crowns!

"I wish I had a dress-up box of my own!" Angelina says. "I would have ballet dresses and fairy wings and a chef's hat. . . ."

That gives Grandma an idea.

The next week Angelina's grandparents come to visit her, and they bring a big wooden box and paint supplies with them. Grandpa covers the kitchen table with an old cloth to protect it and puts everything on top.

"What is that?" Angelina asks.

"Your new dress-up box!" Grandma says. "You can decorate it however you want, and then we'll make clothes to fill it."

"I've always wanted a dress-up box!" Angelina says excitedly. Grandma and Grandpa look at each other and smile.

Angelina has so much fun painting and decorating her box.

"Ta-da!" she says, when it's all done.

"Lovely, Angelina," says Grandma.

"Good job!" says Grandpa.

Grandma takes Angelina to Mrs. Thimble's General Store to pick out fabric, buttons, ribbons, thread, patterns, and more.

"We're making clothes for my new dress-up box!" Angelina tells Mrs. Thimble.

Mrs. Thimble gives her some pretty fabric pieces. "You can keep these in your box to make a skirt or a gown or whatever you can imagine!"

"Thank you!" Angelina says.

Now every time Angelina's grandparents come over, they help Angelina make dress-up costumes. Grandma shows Angelina how to cut a pattern, thread a needle, and sew buttons onto fabric.

When they finally finish making all the costumes, Grandpa puts everything in the dress-up box . . . including the fabric from Mrs. Thimble.

"Thank you, Grandma and Grandpa!" Angelina says, and she gives each of them a big hug. "I love my dress-up box!"

"I wish Alice and Henry could see this!" Angelina tells them.
"We could play dress-up and have a tea party and . . ."
"A dress-up tea party sounds wonderful!" Grandma says.

Grandma and Grandpa talk to Angelina's parents, and they invite Alice and cousin Henry over to Angelina's house. It isn't long before all three mouselings have picked out special dress-up costumes!

"I'm a doctor!" says Alice.
"I'm a ballet dancer!" says Henry.

"I'm a chef!" says Angelina. "Would you like a cheddar-cheese pie or a cheddar-cheese biscuit?"

"One of each, please," Alice replies.

"Me too!" Henry says.

"What's this?" Alice asks, picking up a piece of fabric from Mrs. Thimble.

"It's anything you want it to be," Angelina explains.

Alice takes the fabric and wraps it around herself. "This is my gown. Isn't it pretty?"

Henry puts on a cowboy hat and says, "I'm a cowboy, and this is my lasso!"

Angelina adds pretty fabric to her ballet costume and says, "Look! Now I'm Super Angelina Ballerina!"

Angelina, Alice, and Henry help Grandma set the table. Angelina's mother, father, and baby sister come down to join in the fun.

"We heard there was a dress-up tea party happening," Angelina's mother says.

Angelina's father bows, and says, "Princess Angelina Ballerina Fairy, I presume?"

They all sit down for a delicious tea party.

"Thank you for the best dress-up tea party ever, Grandma and Grandpa!" says Angelina.

"You're very welcome, Princess Angelina Ballerina Fairy!" Grandpa and Grandma say, smiling.

Dancing Day

Angelina Ballerina loves ballet so much that as soon as she wakes up in the morning, she can't wait to start dancing.

"Today is a dancing day!" Angelina announces to her doll, Mousie.

While Angelina brushes her teeth, she practices her pliés!

And while Angelina eats her breakfast of pancakes and berries, she practices pointing her toes!

When it is time for school, Angelina leaps . . . and turns . . . and twirls across the schoolyard!

At Miss Lilly's Ballet School, Angelina practices pirouettes with the class.

"Remember to begin in fifth position," says Miss Lilly, "keep your head level, and point your toes."

Angelina does a few pirouettes. At first she is a little wobbly, but she tries again.

"Lovely, Angelina!" Miss Lilly says.

Angelina's family has a big surprise for her when they come to pick her up from Miss Lilly's Ballet School: They are taking her to see a real ballet!

The ballet dancers move so gracefully, they look like they are floating across the stage.

"Their pirouettes are *soooo* beautiful!" Angelina whispers.

At the end of the show, Angelina even gets to go backstage to give a rose to Serena Silvertail, the prima ballerina!

"You're my favorite ballerina," Angelina tells Serena. "When I grow up, I want to be just like you!"

"If you practice every day, you can do anything!" says Serena Silvertail.

Serena Silvertail kindly signs
a pair of her ballet slippers for
Angelina to have as a keepsake!
"Thank you!" Angelina says
with a curtsy.

At home that night, Angelina and her family eat a delicious dinner of cheddar-cheese pies.

"My pie looks like a rose!" Angelina says, noticing the decoration on top.

Before her mother baked the pies, Angelina's father arranged pieces of pastry dough to look like rose petals!

"It's a rose for *our* favorite ballerina," her mother says.

"It's so pretty . . . and yummy, too!" Angelina says.

Angelina brushes her teeth and puts on her pajamas, and then she proudly hangs Serena Silvertail's ballet slippers in a place of honor in her bedroom. Angelina's father reads her a bedtime story about ballerinas, and Angelina's mother gives her a pink tutu she made for Mousie.

"Today was a wonderful dancing day," Angelina says, "and it was a wonderful family day, too!" Angelina gives her parents an enormous hug.

"That is the best kind of day," her mother whispers.

"Sweet dreams, Angelina," her father says.

Angelina falls asleep and dreams the best kind of dreams . . . dreams of dancing with Serena Silvertail!

Big Dreams!

It was a beautiful morning in Chipping Cheddar, and Angelina had to get ready for ballet class at Miss Lilly's Dance School, but she was still fast asleep!

"Good morning, Angelina. It's time to wake up . . . ," said Mrs. Mouseling. Then she noticed the pile of clothes and toys on the floor of Angelina's bedroom. "My goodness!" Mrs. Mouseling gasped.

"What's wrong?" Angelina asked as she rubbed her eyes.

"Your room is a mess, Angelina!" Mrs. Mouseling exclaimed. "You need to put everything away before ballet school."

"Can't I clean up after class?" Angelina asked.

"There is no time like the present!" Mrs. Mouseling said.

Angelina got right to work. She really didn't want to be late for ballet class!

First Angelina made her bed. Then she carefully gathered her stuffed animals and set them on the wooden chest by the window.

She picked up her toys, and she hung up the clothes she had left on the floor.

Angelina had almost finished putting things away when she noticed a small book under her bed.

Angelina squealed with joy! "*My Book of Ballet Dreams*," Angelina said, reading the title aloud. "I thought I lost this!" She hugged the book close.

Angelina's parents helped her make the book when she first decided she wanted to be a ballerina. They always encouraged Angelina to work hard and follow her dreams.

Angelina started looking though the pages and remembering all the things she used to only *dream* of!

Angelina's first dream was to have a pair of ballet shoes. She remembered the day when her parents surprised her with pink ballet slippers. She was so excited that she never wanted to take them off, and she practiced dancing anywhere she could!

After Angelina went to her first ballet class, she dreamed of perfecting all the different ballet positions. Miss Lilly was an excellent ballet teacher, and Angelina learned all the positions very quickly.

Then Angelina dreamed of doing her first arabesque . . . and one day, after lots of practicing, she did it alongside her best friend, Alice! Alice always encouraged Angelina to keep trying, even when things were challenging.

One of Angelina's biggest dreams was getting her first lead role in a performance! She worked really hard and practiced every day so she could dance as Cindermouse . . . and she did it!

Angelina turned to the last page of her book and read, "'Prima ballerina!'" One day she hoped to be a star ballerina

just like her idol, Serena Silvertail!

"I'm still working on that one," Angelina said, "so I better finish cleaning up my room. I won't become a prima ballerina if I miss ballet class!"

Mrs. Mouseling came back to Angelina's bedroom just as Angelina finished cleaning up.

"Well done, Angelina!" Mrs. Mouseling said. "Are you ready for breakfast and ballet class?"

"Ready!" Angelina said. She grabbed her ballet bag and tucked her book inside.

Angelina showed Miss Lilly her book as soon as she arrived at ballet class.

"It's wonderful!" Miss Lilly said. "Next week I'll bring some paper and crayons, and we can all make books about our big ballerina dreams."

"Dreaming is only the first step!" Angelina said.